This book belongs to:

Rain, Rain, Come Again

Disney's Out & About With Pooh
A Grow and Learn Library

Published by Advance Publishers
© 1996 Disney Enterprises, Inc.
Based on the Pooh stories by A. A. Milne © The Pooh Properties Trust.
All rights reserved. Printed in the United States.
No part of this book may be reproduced or copied in any form
without written permission from the copyright owner.

Written by Ann Braybrooks
Illustrated by Arkadia Illustration Ltd.
Designed by Vickey Bolling
Produced by Bumpy Slide Books

ISBN:1-885222-68-8
10 9 8 7 6 5 4 3 2

For days and days, Pooh and some of his friends had been planning an Explore. First they had decided to explore the North Pole, but since Pooh had already discovered *that,* they decided to go as far as they could and find a place that no one — including them — had ever seen, which they would name Pooh-Piglet-Roo Land.

During one planning meeting, Eeyore wandered by and looked so gloomy that Pooh said, "Eeyore, why don't you come with us? Instead of discovering Pooh-Piglet-Roo Land, we'll look for Pooh-Piglet-Roo-Eeyore Land."

Eeyore thought for a moment. "It does have a nice ring to it," he said finally. "I accept."

When the big day arrived, Pooh and Piglet and Roo went to Eeyore's house, carrying their map and compass and treasure buckets. But Eeyore wouldn't come outside.

"The sky looks kind of gray," he said. "We certainly can't go on an Explore if it's going to rain."

"Rain?" repeated Roo, looking worried. "Oh, dear."

"It may rain, and it may not," Pooh answered cheerfully. "You never can tell with weather."

"Pooh," Roo began, "if we get caught in the rain, won't the water fall on my head?"

"Yes, I suppose it will," Pooh answered.
"But I don't like water on my head or in my eyes," Roo explained. "Not even when Mama gives me a bath."

"Well, if it does rain, we can just turn our buckets upside down and wear them as hats," Pooh suggested.

"Or we could put the map over us, like this," Piglet said. He gave one edge to Roo to hold, and together they stood underneath it.

"Well, all right then," Roo agreed reluctantly. And so the explorers set out to find Pooh-Piglet-Roo-Eeyore Land, come rain or shine.

As they reached the middle of a large, open field, the rain *did* come.

"I told you so!" cried Eeyore as the friends ran for shelter beneath some trees.

"My bucket!" called Roo, as his homemade rain hat went flying into the air with every bounce.

"I wish I had my umbrella," Piglet confessed.

Pooh, meanwhile, was trying to unfold the map.

As they huddled beneath the branches, catching their breath, Pooh held out the soggy paper.

"Oh, bother," he said. "The rain made the ink run on the map, and now we can't read it."

"At least we still have the compass," said Piglet.

"No, we don't," confessed Roo. "I dropped it when I was hurrying!"

"I knew this Explore was a bad idea," Eeyore groaned miserably.

Roo looked out at the falling rain. "I'll go search for the compass," he announced bravely.

He closed his eyes and ventured out from under the tree — but luckily, just at that moment, the rain stopped.

The little kangaroo took one hop across the field and found that he could hop no farther.

"Uh-oh! I'm stuck!" he exclaimed. "The rain left the ground all muddy!"

But when Roo finally pulled his feet out of the muck, a big smile crossed his face.

"Gee, listen to the wonderful noise the mud makes!" he giggled as he went SQUISH SQUISH SQUISH with his feet.

"Come on!" Pooh said to the others. "Let's all try it!"
Pooh hurried over but stopped when he heard
something crunch beneath his foot.
"Oops!" he said. "I think I found the compass."

Pooh picked it up and turned in a circle. "That's funny," he said. "No matter which direction I stand in, the arrow points north."

Eeyore moaned, "Now we'll never find our way back."

"Oh, dear!" said Piglet. "We really *are* lost."

Pooh thought for a while, then heard his tummy rumble. "Ah!" he said. "I almost forgot. I can find the way home just by listening to my tummy. It can *always* hear my honey pots calling."

"If you're hungry, Pooh, I can fix you something to eat,"
said Roo.

He scooped up some wonderful, gooey mud and put it in his bucket. Then he took out a handful and began patting it into shape.

"I'll make you some mud pies," he announced. Then he picked up some little rocks and said, "With raisins in them, too!"

Roo bent down to pick up another rock. "Yikes!" he
said. "There are baby snakes under here!"

"Those aren't snakes," said Pooh, who was quite relieved. "Those are earthworms. They come out after the rain."

"Ooo," said Roo. "They're slimy!"

"I've been thinking," Pooh said, looking around. "Since we've never been *here* before, perhaps this is Pooh-Piglet-Roo-Eeyore Land."

Eeyore gazed around the muddy field. "Somehow," he said, "I thought it would be grander."

"I didn't think there would be worms," said Piglet.

"I didn't imagine it to be so wet," added Roo.

"We'll keep looking, then," said Pooh, who wasn't and fell into a great big puddle.

"Here, let me help," offered Piglet, who instantly fell in.

Soon Eeyore and Piglet both slipped in, too. Since they were already wet, the friends decided to enjoy a game of puddle-jumping.

"Whee!" cried Roo, who was having so much fun he didn't seem to notice the water splashing on his head.

When they had finished, Piglet looked up and said,
"Look! Over there! I see a cloud that looks like a hat."
"And I see a bee," added Eeyore.
"Where?" Pooh exclaimed. "I don't hear any buzzing."

"Not a *real* bee, Pooh," sniffed Eeyore. "A *cloud* bee."

"Oh, bother," said Pooh, disappointed. "My tummy's rumbling."

"You should have tried some of my mud pies," said Roo.

As they continued their search for Pooh-Piglet-Roo-Eeyore Land, the explorers found some blueberry bushes still glistening from the rain.

Pooh popped a berry into his mouth. "Umm," he said. "A bear's got to keep his strength up if he's to go exploring."

"Delicious!" said Roo, smacking his lips.
Everyone agreed that the rain made the berries taste
extra juicy, so they filled their buckets to the brim.

A little while later, as Pooh's tummy led them closer to home, the friends came across some footprints in the mud. "You don't suppose they belong to a heffalump," wondered Piglet.

"I don't know if they come out after a rain," Pooh answered.

"They should!" exclaimed Roo. "The rain is fun!"

"If you like that sort of thing," said Eeyore, who secretly did.

Quickly, quietly, the explorers followed the tracks, keeping an eye out for heffalumps, woozles, and other wild animals — just in case.

When the tracks ended, they were standing at Pooh's front door.

"Do we have to go in?" Piglet asked.

"If there's a heffalump inside," Pooh whispered, "I've got to stop him before he eats all of my honey."

With his friends gathered cautiously behind him, Pooh pushed open the door

"Hello!" said Kanga when they were inside. "I was sure your Explore got ruined by the rain, so I made you all some tea and cookies to make you feel better."

"But our Explore didn't get ruined," said Roo breathlessly. "We made mud pies and went puddle-jumping and picked berries and everything!"

The happy travelers joined Kanga for tea, all the while planning their next Explore, during which they might find the real Pooh-Piglet-Roo-Eeyore Land.

"Maybe," suggested Eeyore, "we could do it on a rainy day again." And everyone agreed that was a splendid idea.

Then Roo stretched and said, "Mama, may I have a nice bath before I go to bed?"

Kanga just smiled and kissed the top of his head.